This book belongs to

----

withdrawn
From
stock

D1150120

Bluebell Glade

Dandelion Dell

Heart of Misty Wood

Hawthorn Hedgerows

Heather Hill

Sundown Hill

Golden Meadow

Crystal Cave

Moonshine Pond

Dewdrop Spring

Honeydew Meadow

Mulberry Bushes

Misty Wood Rabbit Warren

HOME SWEET HOME

How many **Fairy Animals** books have you collected?

Chloe the Kitten

Bella the Bunny

Paddy the Puppy

Mia the Mouse

✓ Hailey the Hedgehog

Sophie the Squirrel

Poppy the Pony

Betsy the Bunny

Daisy the Deer

Katie the Kitten

Polly the Puppy

Paige the Pony

Fairy Animals

of Misty Wood

Hailey the Hedgehog

Lily Small

EGMONT

With special thanks to Liss Norton

EGMONT
We bring stories to life

Hailey the Hedgehog first published in Great Britain 2013
by Egmont UK Limited
The Yellow Building, 1 Nicholas Road, London W11 4AN

Text copyright © 2013 Hothouse Fiction Ltd
Illustrations copyright © 2013 Kirsteen Harris Jones
All rights reserved

ISBN 978 1 4052 6660 4

www.egmont.co.uk

www.hothousefiction.com

www.fairyanimals.com

A CIP catalogue record for this title is available from the British Library

Printed and bound in Great Britain by The CPI Group

54739/3

All rights reserved. No part of this publication may be reproduced, stored in a retrieval system,
or transmitted, in any form or by any means, electronic, mechanical, photocopying, recording
or otherwise, without the prior permission of the publisher and copyright owner.

Stay safe online. Any website addresses listed in this book are correct at the time of going to
print. However, Egmont is not responsible for content hosted by third parties. Please be aware
that online content can be subject to change and websites can contain content that is unsuitable
for children. We advise that all children are supervised when using the internet.

MIX
Paper
FSC FSC® C018306

CORK CITY

9797647

LIBRARIES

Contents

CHAPTER ONE

Parade Day!

Winter had come to Misty Wood and the fairy animals were very excited – today was the day of the Christmas Parade!

Hailey, a tiny hedgehog, lay

in her cosy bed of moss, listening to the wind outside singing through the trees. She pulled her blanket of velvety dock leaves up to her nose.

'I do love winter,' Hailey said with a sigh. As she pictured the wind blowing the last of the golden leaves from the branches, and the woods twinkling with frost, she started to smile.

'Are you up, Hailey?' her dad

2

called from the far end of their
burrow.

'Nearly,' Hailey called back.
She jumped out of bed, licked her
tiny pink paws and gave her face a
quick wash. Then she checked her
dandelion clock. 'Yay!' she cried.
'It's breakfast time!'

When she got to the other
end of the burrow her dad was
busy chopping acorns. 'Morning,
Hailey,' he said. 'I'm making you

some acorn porridge – to keep
you nice and warm out there. The
woods are going to need a lot of
tidying up before the parade.'

'Great!' Hailey exclaimed.
'I love having lots of leaves to
collect.' She fluttered her silver
and red wings excitedly, sending
sparkles of glittering light around
the burrow.

Hailey was a Hedgerow
Hedgehog. Like all the other fairy

animals, she had a special job
to do to help make Misty Wood
a wonderful place to live. The
Hedgerow Hedgehogs' job was to
collect fallen leaves on their prickly
spines, to keep the woods neat and
tidy. That was why Hailey loved
winter so much. There were so
many colourful leaves to gather,
especially on a windy day like this.

Dad finished making the
porridge and poured it into three

HAILEY THE HEDGEHOG

nutshell bowls. Hailey took hers
and went to sit on a pebble stool in
the corner. Just as she ate her first
mouthful, a gust of cold air came
whisking through the burrow.

'It's only me,' a voice called.
Hailey's mum hurried inside. Her
paws were full of mistletoe sprigs.
'Goodness!' she exclaimed. 'What a
wind!' Laying the mistletoe on the
conker table, she smoothed down
the ruffled fur on her face and legs.

'Ooh, is the mistletoe for the Christmas Parade?' Hailey asked. She could hardly wait for the parade to start. It took place every year. All the fairy animals dressed up in beautiful leaves and berries and marched through Misty Wood behind the Moss Mouse pipe and drum band. Afterwards, everyone visited the nests and burrows of their friends to admire their decorations and to share a tasty

nibble or an acorn cup of warm
cranberry juice.

'Yes,' her mum replied. 'I'm
using mistletoe and holly this
year.' She turned round and
Hailey saw that her mum's prickles
were stuck all over with shiny red
holly berries.

'I'll string them together
to make garlands,' her mum
continued. She shook the berries
from her spines and pushed them

into a tidy pile beside the fire.

Hailey couldn't stop smiling as she pictured herself wearing a beautiful red and white garland. In fact, she was grinning so much that some porridge trickled out of

the corner of her mouth! Hailey
quickly licked it up with her velvety
pink tongue.

'Here's your breakfast,' said
Hailey's dad, passing her mum a
bowl of porridge. 'And I'm making
my special chestnut pudding for
after the parade.'

'Yippee!' Hailey cheered.
That was another good thing
about winter – there were always
chestnuts to be found, and Dad's

chestnut pudding was *delicious*!

Hailey ate her porridge quickly. Every day she made sure that Misty Wood was spick and span, but today – parade day – she was determined to be extra careful. Today, she wouldn't leave a single leaf out of place. And she had to be home earlier than usual, too, so she'd have time to dress up.

'I'm off then,' she said, as soon as her bowl was empty.

'Don't forget that the parade begins at one o'clock, Hailey,' her mum reminded her.

'I won't,' Hailey said with a smile. There was *no way* she was going to miss her favourite event!

Spreading her wings, she fluttered up the long passageway that led out of her warm burrow and into Hawthorn Hedgerows, which grew at the very edge of Misty Wood.

As soon as Hailey got above ground she could see that the wind had been busy. Only a few leaves still clung to the twigs above her head. They fluttered as the wind danced around them, whistling its winter tune.

They'll be off soon, too, thought Hailey, smiling. *And then I'll have even more leaves to tidy.*

She flitted out from under the hedgerow and gasped in delight.

Jack Frost had been at work during the night, sprinkling his glittering ice crystals across the grass. The crystals shimmered pink, blue and silver in the wintry sunshine, and each blade of grass stood up stiff and straight no matter how hard the wind blew.

Hailey gazed around. '*Beautiful,*' she breathed. She fluttered up into the air and spread her wings wide so the wind would lift her high.

She wanted to look at the grassy
spaces between the hedgerows.
'I'll start collecting leaves in the
messiest patch,' she said to herself.

Up, up, up she soared into
the clear blue sky. Soon, Misty
Wood was spread out beneath her

like a colourful patchwork quilt.

The frosted grass glinted silver.

Dewdrop Spring was the same

bright blue as the sky, with spots

of shiny ice here and there. And

the patch of snowdrops beside it

looked as clean and white as a

fluffy cloud.

Further on still, Moonshine Pond shone pearly-blue, full of glowing moonbeans, and beyond that was the pretty, vivid purple of Heather Hill.

Right in the centre of every-thing was a patch of deep, dark green – the mysterious Heart of Misty Wood, where the Wise Wishing Owl lived. Hailey had never seen the Wise Wishing Owl,

but she had heard lots of stories about her wisdom. And everyone said that she had the power to grant wishes.

As Hailey looked around, she spotted a patch of leaf-strewn grass not far from her burrow. She quickly fluttered down. 'Perfect!' she cried happily, puffing out her spikes. 'Now I'm ready to start work!'

CHAPTER TWO

Hungry Hugo!

Tucking her nose and legs in against her tummy, and folding her glittering wings, Hailey curled herself into a tight ball. Then she rolled to and fro across the frosty

grass, gathering the leaves on her

prickles.

Soon the patch of grass was

clear. Hailey scurried over to a

nearby hedge and shook herself. The leaves fluttered down from her spines and she scooped them into a tidy heap at the base of the hedge. Smiling, she looked across the spotless grass. 'Good job!' she congratulated herself. 'Now, on to the next one.'

She unfurled her wings and flew further into the woods.

Soon, she came to a grove where the Holly Hamsters were

22

hard at work. They were nibbling
the glossy holly leaves into their
beautiful curved shapes.

'Hello, Holly Hamsters!'
Hailey called as she fluttered past.

'Hello, Hailey!' they called
back, their chubby cheeks bulging.

Just beyond the holly grove
was an ancient chestnut tree with
twisted branches and a huge, fat
trunk. Leaves were scattered all
around it and Hailey swooped

23

down eagerly to gather them up.

As she rolled to and fro, collecting the leaves, she made up a little song:

'I love winter when the wild

wind blows,

Scattering the leaves all

around, all around,

Even though it chills my nose

and toes

When I roll on the frosty

ground.'

Suddenly she heard a small voice. 'I hate winter,' it said. 'I don't know why you're singing about it. It's the worst season of the whole year!'

Hailey stopped rolling and uncurled herself. She looked around in surprise. How could anybody hate winter?

A teeny-tiny Holly Hamster with pale brown fur and yellow wings was crouched on the edge

of the holly grove. His head and wings were drooping miserably. Hailey recognised him – his name was Hugo.

'Whatever's the matter, Hugo?' asked Hailey.

'I've ruined my holly bush,' he replied, looking up sadly. 'And now it's going to look horrible for the Christmas Parade. Every fairy animal in the whole wood will march past here and see what I've done.'

Hailey fluttered over to him.

'Perhaps it's not as bad as you . . .'

She fell silent as she spotted the

bush. 'Oh, dear.'

The bush was almost

completely bare, with every leaf

nibbled right down to the stem.

27

Hailey stared at Hugo. 'What happened to it?'

'I was hungry,' Hugo said. 'And the leaves were so yummy I couldn't stop eating them.' He peered up at Hailey dreamily. 'Honestly, they were the most delicious things I've ever tasted – even more delicious than chestnuts!' He sat back on the ground and gave a loud burp.

Hailey's tummy rumbled as

28

she thought of her dad's chestnut pudding. It was hard to imagine anything tasting nicer. They must have been very tasty leaves indeed!

'Maybe I should try digging up the whole bush,' Hugo said. 'Then I could hide it.' The tiny hamster leaped up and began scratching at the soil around the bush's roots.

'No, Hugo!' Hailey cried. 'Don't do that.' She rubbed her

29

nose thoughtfully. 'I think I know what to do,' she said at last.

Hugo looked at her hopefully, his dark eyes shining. 'Really?'

'Wait here a moment,' said Hailey. She fluttered back to the chestnut tree and quickly rolled over the last of the leaves to stick them to her prickles. Then she whooshed back to Hugo.

'Here you go,' she said, shaking the leaves to the ground. 'You can

30

nibble these into holly leaf shapes,
and I'll hang them on the bush.'

Hugo bounced up and down
on his hind legs. 'That's brilliant!
Thanks, Hailey!' he cried.

'Just make sure you don't
gobble them all up this time,'
Hailey said with a grin.

'I won't,' Hugo said, patting
his furry tummy. 'I'm far too full!'
Then he set to work, taking dainty
little bites out of the edges of the

bright chestnut tree leaves.

Hailey twisted the leaf stems around the holly twigs and soon the bush was covered in golden holly-shaped leaves.

'These leaves make my bush

32

look so pretty!' Hugo cried out happily. He hugged Hailey, then leaped back. 'Ouch! I forgot all about your prickles!' he chuckled, rubbing his paws.

'Sorry,' giggled Hailey. 'But I'm glad you're pleased with your *holly* bush.'

'I am!' Hugo exclaimed. Then he looked at the little pile of spare leaves. 'Can you close your eyes for a minute?' he asked Hailey.

'Why?' Hailey said, puzzled.

'I can't tell you yet – it's a surprise.'

Hailey loved surprises. She closed her eyes and listened, trying to work out what Hugo was doing. But all she could hear was the rustle of leaves.

'Ta-da!' cried Hugo, after a few minutes.

Hailey opened her eyes.

'I made this just for you,'

34

Hugo said. He held up a beautiful garland made from all the spare leaves. He slipped it over Hailey's head. 'It's to say thank you for helping me.'

'It's lovely!' Hailey exclaimed. 'Thanks, Hugo. I'll wear it in the Christmas Parade. Ooh, I'd better get going – I've got loads of work to do before then!'

CHAPTER THREE

A Shimmer of Moonbeams

Hailey soared into the air and fluttered quickly over the rabbit warren. Down below, her friend Bella the Bud Bunny was hard at

work opening snowdrop buds with her twitchy nose. Hailey waved, but she didn't fly down to speak to Bella in case it made her late for the parade.

She flew over Dewdrop Spring, then on to Moonshine Pond which shone like a blue pearl in the winter sunshine. 'Ha!' she cried, as she spotted some leaves at the pond's edge.

Hailey flew down to land. She curled into a ball and rolled quickly down the bank, gathering the leaves on her prickles as she went. She sang her song as she rolled faster and faster:

'I love winter when the wild

wind blows,

Scattering the leaves all around,

all around,

Even though it chills my nose

and toes

When I roll on the frosty

ground.'

'I used to love winter, but I most definitely don't any more!' said a gloomy voice.

The voice was coming from

40

a tall pine tree beside the pond. Hailey unrolled quickly, and looked around in surprise. 'Who said that?' she asked.

'Me, Maisie the Moonbeam Mole,' the voice replied softly.

Hailey was very puzzled indeed. Moonbeam Moles never usually came out during the day. They did their special job at night-time – catching moonbeams and scattering them in Moonshine

Pond to make it look pearly and beautiful. During the day they stayed in their burrows and slept – and they certainly didn't go climbing trees! Hailey knew that they woke up specially for the Christmas Parade each year – but it was a bit too early yet.

Hailey fluttered over quickly to investigate.

A pair of tiny brown eyes peeked out from amongst the pine

needles. They looked very tired
and were full of tears.

'What's wrong, Maisie?'
Hailey gasped. 'And why are you
still awake?'

'I've been here since night-
time,' Maisie sniffed sadly. 'My
net's caught in this tree and I can't
pull it free.' She crept along a
branch and pointed up to the top
of the tree with a trembling paw.

Hailey saw something glowing

43

HAILEY THE HEDGEHOG

amongst the branches. It was the net – crammed full of twinkling moonbeams. It had got tangled around some pinecones.

'I can't put my moonbeams into the pond,' Maisie gulped, 'so it won't look lovely for the Christmas Parade.'

'But it *does* look lovely,' Hailey told her. 'I noticed it when I was flying this way. It looks like a beautiful pearl.' She patted the

tiny mole's shoulder, trying to make her feel better.

'Not my bit of the pond,' sobbed Maisie. She pointed to a patch of water close to the bank. Now Hailey understood why Maisie was so upset. The water there was dark and still, with not even a hint of glistening moonlight.

Hailey thought hard. 'I know what to do!' she cried. 'I'll hook my prickles through your net. Then I'll

be able to fly up and lift it clear
of those pinecones.'

Maisie stopped crying
and gazed hopefully at Hailey.
'Do you think it will work?' she
whispered.

'There's only one way to find
out,' said Hailey.

She soared to the top of
the tree, then fluttered round it,
hooking the net over her prickles.
'Here goes,' she called. Flapping

47

her wings hard, she flew higher
still. Part of the net came free and
some pinecones dropped to the
ground.

'It's working!' squealed Maisie
happily.

Hailey flapped her wings
harder than ever. More pinecones
dropped down and now most of
the net was free. 'One more go,'
Hailey panted. Using all of her
strength, she zoomed into the air

and suddenly the net was dangling
free below her. The moonbeams
twinkled as they swung from side
to side.

'Hurray!' Hailey cheered.
She flew to the ground with the
heavy net.

Maisie fluttered down beside
her, her lilac wings shimmering in
the sunshine. 'Thank you, thank
you,' she cried. Her tiny eyes
shone with relief as she unhooked

49

the net from Hailey's spines. 'Now the pond will look perfect for the parade!'

Scooping out a pawful of moonbeams, Maisie tossed them into the patch of dark water. They plopped down out of sight, then rose to the surface and their beautiful pearly light rippled out, making the water gleam.

'That looks beautiful, Maisie,' breathed Hailey, flying up to see

the pond from above.

'All because of you,' replied
Maisie. She reached into her net
and took out the last glowing
moonbeam. 'May I give you a
present to thank you for helping

me?' she asked shyly.

'Oh, yes please!' Hailey cried.
She loved presents!

Maisie placed the moonbeam
on the biggest leaf in Hailey's
garland. Hailey watched
entranced as gold and silver
sparkles spread from leaf to leaf.
Soon the whole garland was
twinkling brightly.

'Thank you!' gasped Hailey,
astonished. She'd never seen

anything so beautiful before. It
was as though she was wearing
a necklace made of glittering
moonlight.

'No, thank *you*, Hailey,'
Maisie said. 'If you hadn't helped
me, the pond wouldn't have looked

its best for the Christmas Parade.'

'The Parade!' Hailey cried, remembering how much she had to do before it began. 'I must go! Bye, Maisie.'

CHAPTER FOUR

A Starry Surprise

Hailey fluttered up into the air
and headed for the trees that grew
in the Heart of Misty Wood. She
could see a few untidy leaves on
the grass there. As she drew near,

she started to sing her winter song:

'I love winter when the wild

wind blows –'

'Well, I don't!' boomed a cross

voice. It was coming from behind a

tree at the very back of the Heart

of Misty Wood.

Hailey peeped round the tree

trunk nervously, wondering who it

could be.

Boris, one of the Bark

Badgers, was hunched on the

56

frosty ground. He was frowning at his paw.

'What's wrong, Boris?' Hailey asked. The Bark Badgers carved beautiful patterns into tree trunks with their strong claws. They were usually very kind and helpful. Hailey had never seen one looking so grumpy before.

'I'm supposed to be carving wintry patterns into the bark of the trees around here,' Boris replied.

'I wanted everything to be perfect for the parade, so I flew up on to a branch to reach further up the trunk. But the branch was slippery with frost and I fell down.' He held up his paw and Hailey saw that it was sore and swollen. 'Now my paw's so painful that I can't do my job,' he sighed.

'Poor you,' Hailey said. She wondered what she could do to help him.

'I should have been more careful!' Boris said glumly. 'Now when the parade comes past here the fairy animals won't be thinking happy, Christmassy thoughts. They'll be thinking, look

at those plain old trees!'

Suddenly they heard some loud barking and looked round, startled. A group of Pollen Puppies came scampering along, their ears flopping around and their tongues hanging out with excitement.

'Hey! Aren't you coming to the Christmas Parade?' the puppies woofed, wagging their tails and scattering specks of golden pollen all around.

'Is it time?' Hailey asked

them anxiously.

'Nearly,' one of the puppies

woofed. 'And we don't want to be

late!'

'Neither do I!' gulped Hailey,

as the playful pups went bounding away. Her mind started whirring. She couldn't leave poor Boris looking so unhappy. Maybe she could help him, *and* make it back home in time for the start of the parade . . .

'Let me help,' Hailey said. 'My spines are nearly as sharp as a badger's claws. If you tell me what to do, perhaps I can carve the tree trunks for you.'

Boris's face broke into a cheery smile. 'That would be wonderful!' he exclaimed.

Hailey flew up and pressed her prickles against the first tree. 'OK, I'm ready,' she said. 'Tell me what to do.'

'Go up a bit,' called Boris.

Hailey fluttered upwards. She felt her spines cutting through the tree's bark. 'I think it's working!' she cried excitedly.

63

'Now right a bit,' Boris said, beaming.

Hailey flew right.

'Left, then down,' called Boris.

Hailey followed all of Boris's instructions.

'That's it,' he said at last. 'The first tree's finished. Let's see if it worked.'

Hailey turned to look at the tree trunk. 'Oh!' she gasped. 'How pretty!' Her spines had

A STARRY SURPRISE

carved a pattern of beautiful lacy

snowflakes cascading from the sky.

'Next tree!' declared Boris.

'Quick!'

Hailey worked at top speed,

and soon she'd carved snowflake

patterns into all of Boris's trees.

'I'd better go home now,' she said,

as she turned to admire the last

carved trunk.

'Hold on, there's just one more

thing to do,' said Boris, holding

up a piece of smooth bark that
had been gnawed into a diamond
shape. Hurriedly, Hailey pressed
her spines against it and moved in
the directions Boris told her.

'There,' he said. 'All done.' He
held up the bark to show Hailey
and she saw that she'd carved a
beautiful star.

'Lovely!' she exclaimed.

'It's for you,' Boris said. 'To
thank you for all your help.' He

hung it right in the middle of her

glowing leaf garland.

'Thank you!' cried Hailey.

'And now I must fly! Bye, Boris.'

She made up her mind to go

straight home. 'If I stop and pick

up any more leaves I won't have

68

time to get ready for the parade,'
she said to herself.

Her red and silver wings
fluttered furiously as she sped
along. She raced past a tree
hung with balls of white-berried
mistletoe. It reminded her of the
decorations her mum was making
and she flapped her wings harder.

Just as she was approaching
Dandelion Dell she spotted some
leaves scattered messily on the

ground beneath a large oak tree.

'Oh, dear!' Hailey squeaked.
The parade would be coming
this way and everyone would see
them. *I'll pick them up quickly*, she
thought to herself, *then I'll rush
straight home. I should still be on time.*

Hurriedly, she flew down,
then curled up tight and began to
roll this way and that, gathering
the leaves. As soon as she started
doing her job she stopped worrying

about being late and started

singing her wintry song again:

>*I love winter when the wild*
>
>*wind blows,*
>
>*Scattering the leaves all around,*
>
>*all around,*
>
>*Even though it chills my nose*
>
>*and toes*
>
>*When I roll on the frosty*
>
>*ground.'*

'How can you sing at a time

like this?' a voice called from a tree

high above her.

Hailey stopped singing and uncurled quickly. 'A time like what?' she replied, fluttering upwards.

'A time as terrible and horrible and awful as this!' the voice wailed.

CHAPTER FIVE

Acorn Disaster!

Hailey flew in closer to the tree.
A beautiful silver Stardust Squirrel
with cute tufty ears was crouched
miserably on a branch. A broken
basket sat beside her.

'Are you all right?' Hailey

asked anxiously.

'No,' huffed the squirrel. 'I am

actually all *wrong*!'

'Oh, dear.' Hailey scratched

her head with a tiny pink paw.

74

'What's the matter?'

The squirrel sighed and twitched her bushy tail, sending a puff of glittery stardust into the air. 'Are you sure you want to know?' she said, looking at Hailey and tilting her head to one side.

Hailey nodded.

'It's a very sad story,' said the squirrel. 'It's so sad it might even make you cry.'

'Oh, err, that's all right,' said

Hailey, bravely.

'OK then.' The squirrel clasped her front paws together. 'Once upon a time, there was a very beautiful Stardust Squirrel called Sabrina – that's me,' she added.

Hailey nodded and smiled.

'And one day – today, actually – Sabrina's mummy sent her out to fetch some acorns to decorate the delicious cake that

she's making for the Christmas Parade. So Sabrina did as she was told, because as well as being beautiful she's a very good little Stardust Squirrel. She filled her basket right to the brim. But then disaster struck!' Sabrina stared at her basket sadly. 'Her basket broke and the acorns went all over the ground.' Sabrina looked at Hailey. 'Isn't that the saddest story you've ever heard?'

Hailey nodded solemnly. 'Yes, it is a very sad story,' she said. 'But maybe I can help you give it a happy ending.'

Sabrina's eyes lit up. 'How?'

Hailey fluttered over and examined the basket. It was woven from stems of dried grass, but some of them had broken and there was a hole in the bottom.

'Let's try putting some leaves over the hole,' suggested

78

Hailey. 'That might do the trick.'
She shook some leaves from her
prickles, then carefully pressed a
few on the bottom of the basket.

'Ooh, that looks a lot better,'
Sabrina said, twitching her tail

excitedly. 'You can't see the hole at all now.'

Hailey and Sabrina flew down to the ground. There were acorns scattered all over the grass and they scampered around picking them up. Then Sabrina dropped them into the basket.

'Here goes,' she said, lifting it.

For a moment it looked as though the repair was strong enough, but then the acorns and

leaves fell through the hole and
rolled across the grass again.

'Oh, no!' Sabrina groaned.
'Now my story's going to have an
even sadder ending!'

'Don't worry, I know how
we can definitely make it happy,'
Hailey said.

Sabrina frowned at her.
'How?'

'I'll collect them with my
prickles. I'm sure they'll pick up

81

acorns just as well as they pick up leaves from the ground.'

Sabrina looked doubtful. 'There's an awful lot of them.'

'Well, I've got an awful lot of prickles!' Hailey giggled. She curled into a ball and began to roll. Soon all the acorns were stuck to her prickles, along with the rest of the fallen leaves.

'Come on, let's get these to your mum,' Hailey said. 'We'll have

to hurry. The parade will be starting soon and we mustn't miss it.'

'Thank you!' Sabrina cried. 'Now my story will have a very happy ending indeed!'

They flew at top speed through the trees, dodging between the branches. 'There!' said Sabrina at last, as a large nest came into view. It was made of sticks, dried grass and leaves, and it was wedged into the fork where two branches joined

83

the trunk of a tall beech tree. They landed on a large branch.

'If you don't mind, I'll put the acorns just here,' said Hailey. 'I've got to go home to get ready.'

'That will be great,' Sabrina replied. 'I can easily roll them into our nest from here.'

Hailey shook her prickles. A few of the acorns came tumbling off, but most of them stayed put.

'Hang on, I'll get them off,'

said Sabrina. Grabbing an acorn, she pulled with all her might. 'I'm not hurting you, am I, Hailey?' she asked.

Hailey could feel the tug on her spines but it wasn't sore. 'No, it's OK, pull as hard as you can!'

Sabrina pulled and pulled and then, finally . . . pop! . . . the acorn came away from Hailey's spine.

'Hurray,' cheered Hailey and Sabrina together.

'Now I *know* I'm strong
enough to get them off,' said
Sabrina proudly. 'I'll be as quick
as I can, so you're not late for
the parade.' One by one, Sabrina

yanked the acorns from Hailey's spines. 'That's the lot!' she panted at last. 'And a good job too. I'm puffed out!'

'Phew!' Hailey sighed with relief. 'Now, I must fly home as *fast* as my wings can take me!'

'Just a minute,' Sabrina said as Hailey was about to flutter into the air. She flew up above Hailey and flicked her tail. Twinkling silver stardust showered down

on Hailey. 'That's to say thank you for helping me,' Sabrina said with a smile.

'Wow!' Hailey gasped, twisting her head to look at her spines. They were twinkling like stars. 'Thanks, Sabrina. That looks amazing!' Hailey flew up into the air. 'See you at the parade,' she called as she sped off through the trees. 'If I get there in time . . .' she whispered to herself.

CHAPTER SIX

An Unexpected Guest

Hailey flew faster than she'd ever
flown before. Misty Wood raced
by in a blur, but at last she saw
Hawthorn Hedgerows.

Zooming towards the
ground, she saw all the Hedgerow
Hedgehogs outside her burrow.
They were dressed in beautiful
garlands made of berries, acorns

and golden leaves, ready for the
Christmas Parade.

Hailey's mum and dad were
amongst them, decked out in
bright holly berries and mistletoe.

91

They were looking around the crowd anxiously. Their eyes lit up in relief when they saw Hailey swishing through the air towards them.

'Where have you been?' Hailey's mum asked as she landed.

'Sorry,' Hailey panted, 'I had to help some friends and it made me late. Have I still got time to get dressed up for the parade?'

Suddenly, Hailey noticed that everyone was staring at her, their mouths gaping in astonishment. She began to feel a tiny bit worried.

'What's wrong?' she asked. She wondered if there was still an acorn or two stuck on her prickles.

'Nothing's wrong,' her dad replied. 'You look . . .'

'Wonderful!' her mum finished for him.

'Yes, you do,' the other hedgehogs agreed, crowding round to see her better.

Hailey's neighbours, Henry and Hilda, scurried into their burrow and came back carrying an upturned mushroom cap filled with water that they used as a mirror. 'Here,' they said, setting it down in front of Hailey. 'Take a look at yourself.'

Hailey peered at her reflection.

94

'Oh!' she gasped. Looking back at her was a hedgehog whose fur and prickles twinkled with silver stardust. Around her neck she wore a beautiful leafy garland that shone with pearly moonlight. A diamond-shaped piece of bark carved with a five-pointed star hung from it. Hailey stared and stared. She could hardly believe that the reflection was hers.

'That's the best Christmas

costume I've ever seen!' Hailey's

mum said, giving her a hug.

'We must go!' her dad cried.

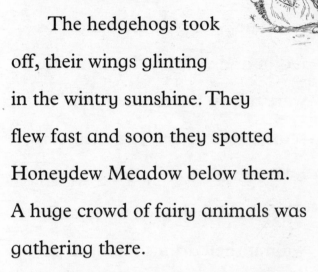

'We don't want the parade
to start without us.'

The hedgehogs took
off, their wings glinting
in the wintry sunshine. They
flew fast and soon they spotted
Honeydew Meadow below them.
A huge crowd of fairy animals was
gathering there.

'Hurray!' cried Hailey. 'We're
not too late after all!'

Hailey, her mum and dad and

all their hedgehog friends fluttered
to the ground and landed gently.

The Moss Mouse band was
ready and waiting. Each mouse
wore a lacy hat nibbled from a
scarlet rosehip and, on their tails,
a bow made from plaited grass.
They held their reed pipes and
walnut shell drums ready to play.
One tiny mouse started beating his
drum eagerly as soon as he saw
Hailey.

'Not yet, Morris,' his mum whispered. 'I'll tell you when to play.'

'Hello, Moss Mice!' Hailey cried. 'You all look so smart!' She could hardly wait for the music to begin.

Hailey's friend Bella the Bunny came hopping over. She was wearing a garland of white snowdrops around each long velvety ear, and one around her

neck. 'Wow, you look fantastic, Hailey!' she cried.

'So do you,' said Hailey. She skipped round in a circle, too excited to keep still for even a moment.

Hailey heard some wings flapping above her head. She looked up eagerly and saw the Stardust Squirrels fluttering down. They were wearing garlands of polished nutshells and their fur

shimmered with silver starlight.
Hailey saw Sabrina and waved.

'Mum's Christmas cake looks
lovely, thanks to you,' Sabrina
called out to her.

Hailey grinned and puffed out
her spikes proudly.

Next, the Cobweb Kittens
arrived, their wings gleaming.

'Look at their costumes!'
gasped Bella. The kittens wore
garlands woven from glistening

cobwebs and hung with bright, glimmering dewdrops.

'Everyone looks wonderful,' Hailey said happily. 'I'm so glad I got here in time.'

Then the cheeky Pollen Puppies came scampering over, wagging their tails in excitement. 'Whoo-hoo for the Christmas Parade!' they barked in chorus. 'Whoo-hoo-woofy-whoo!'

Next, the Bark Badgers came

102

marching past in a line, their silver wings neatly folded. Their black-and-white fur gleamed in the winter sunshine and they wore garlands made from beautifully carved bark shapes.

'And . . . halt!' cried the badger leader. They all stopped marching, and Hailey noticed Boris right at the back.

'Hi, Boris! How's your paw?' she called.

'Not too bad,' he replied. 'It won't stop me from being in the parade!'

Then the Holly Hamsters arrived. Their golden fur shone

brightly, and round their necks they wore garlands of crimson holly berries.

Hugo came trotting over, grinning from ear to ear. 'Just wait till everyone sees my holly bush,' he whispered. 'I bet they've never seen anything like it.' His dark eyes widened suddenly. 'Gosh,' he said, stepping back and gazing at Hailey in astonishment. 'You look beautiful, Hailey.'

Hailey smiled. 'Thanks, Hugo.'

Finally, the Moonbeam Moles appeared. They looked sleepy, but very happy to be there. Garlands of moonbeams hung round their necks, glowing like strings of pearls. Hailey looked over at Maisie and waved her paw. Maisie waved back with a snoozy smile.

Suddenly the crowd fell silent. Hailey heard a gentle rustle from somewhere behind her. Turning,

she saw an enormous bird flying towards Honeydew Meadow from the Heart of Misty Wood. The bird had huge feathery wings that glinted gold in the sunshine. Her brown eyes were big and round and her beak was scarlet.

'Who's that?' asked Hugo and Bella together, looking up in wonder.

Hailey felt a great thrill of excitement and her heart began

to thump. 'I think . . . I think . . .
it's the Wise Wishing Owl!' she
gasped.

CHAPTER SEVEN

The Leader of the Parade

The Wise Wishing Owl was so

beautiful that Hailey could do

nothing but stare as she glided

down into the meadow and folded

HAILEY THE HEDGEHOG

her vast wings. There was silence as the fairy animals waited for her to speak.

A smile spread slowly across the owl's face. 'Is everybody ready for the Christmas Parade?' she called at last. Her voice tinkled like a waterfall splashing over rocks.

'Yes!' cried all the fairy animals together. They looked at each other in delight. The Wise Wishing Owl, the oldest and most

magical creature in Misty Wood, was hardly ever seen. This was a very special day indeed.

'Would you like to lead the parade, Your Wishingness?' asked one of the Bark Badgers.

The owl shook her feathery head. 'Oh, no,' she said. 'One of you should take the lead. I have heard much of the Christmas Parade, and so I have come here to watch.'

112

'Then will you do us the honour of *choosing* the leader for us?' asked the Bark Badger.

'Very well.' The Wise Wishing Owl looked round at all the fairy animals, her snowy white head turning slowly from side to side.

A shiver of delight ran through Hailey as the owl's gaze fell upon her. Never in her wildest dreams had she imagined that she would have the chance to look into the

deep brown eyes of the wonderful
Wise Wishing Owl.

The owl furrowed her feathery
brow. 'It is not an easy choice,'
she said at last. 'You all look very
fine in your leaves and berries,
your starshine and nutshells.
But . . .' She stretched out a huge
wing towards Hailey. 'This little
Hedgerow Hedgehog looks finer
than anything I have ever seen. Will
you lead the parade, my dear?'

114

Hailey gulped. She opened her mouth to reply, but no sound came out.

'Of course she will,' squeaked Bella, nodding at Hailey. 'She would love to!'

Hailey took a deep breath. 'Yes, I'd love to. Thank you, Wise Wishing Owl!' she cried.

'You are welcome,' said the owl kindly.

'And you could start the parade off with your winter song, Hailey,' Hugo piped up.

'Ooh, yes!' squealed Sabrina and Maisie.

All the fairy animals came crowding round. 'We'd love to hear

116

your song, Hailey,' someone called out.

Hailey felt a tiny bit nervous, but she unfurled her wings and fluttered up above the other animals. Then she began to sing:

'I love winter when the wild
wind blows,
Scattering the leaves all around,
all around,
Even though it chills my nose
and toes

When I roll on the frosty

ground.'

As Hailey finished, her

friends clapped and cheered.

Hailey felt like she might burst

with happiness. Then, chattering

excitedly, all the fairy animals

fluttered into line, ready for the

Christmas Parade to begin.

The Hedgerow Hedgehogs

scuttled to line up behind the

band. Behind them were the Bud

Bunnies and the Cobweb Kittens. Then came the Holly Hamsters, the Moonbeam Moles and the Stardust Squirrels. Behind the squirrels, the Bark Badgers marched into position. The Pollen Puppies were right at the back, yapping excitedly and running round in circles as they waited for everyone to move off.

'We're all ready!' cried Hailey from high above. Light bounced off

her beautiful garland and sparkled and danced all around Honeydew Meadow.

The Moss Mouse band began to play a marching song and Hailey felt her toes twitching in time to the music.

'I love winter!' she exclaimed, as she headed to the front of the line. She was so happy that she did a forward roll, picking up a few fallen leaves on her prickles.

'And I *love* Christmas even more!' she called, as she uncurled again. She looked back happily at all her fairy animal friends, waiting eagerly behind her for the parade to start. 'And this is the best Christmas ever!'

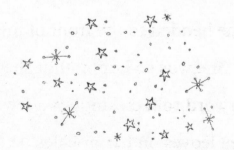

Turn the page for
lots of fun
Misty Wood
activities!

Join the dots

Follow the numbers and join up all the dots to make a lovely picture from the story. Start with dot number 1.

When you've finished joining the dots, you can colour the picture in!

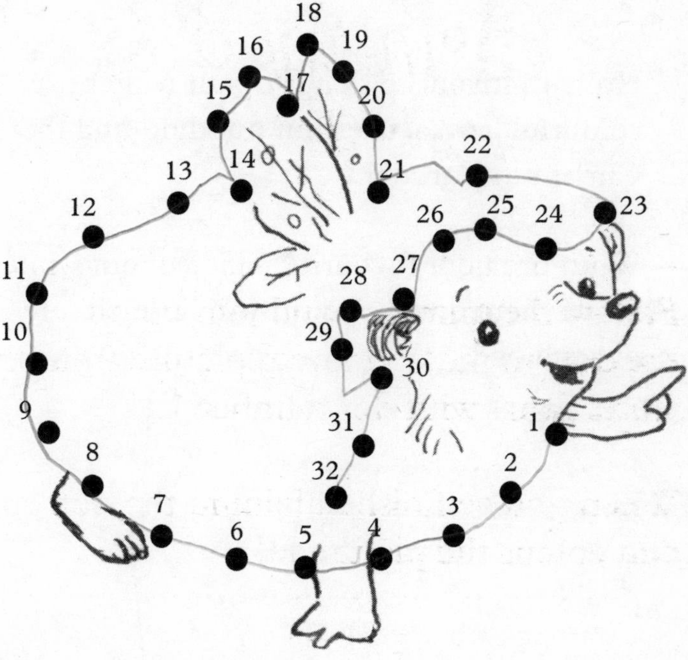
1
2
3
4
5
6
7
8
9
10
11
12
13
14
15
16
17
18
19
20
21
22
23
24
25
26
27
28
29
30
31
32

Winter is wonderful!

Hailey's favourite things about winter are colourful leaves, chestnut pudding and the Christmas Parade!

What are your favourite things about winter? Write them down and draw a little picture of each one.

1. ....

2. ....

3. ....

Help Hugo remember!

Hugo the Holly Hamster likes Hailey's song so much *he* wants to sing it too! But Hugo can't remember all the words. Can you help him? Have a go without looking back at the story!

I love winter when the wild .... blows,

Scattering the .... all around, all around,

Even though it chills my nose and ....

When I roll on the frosty ....

Fairy Animals

of Misty Wood

Meet all the fairy animal friends!

Lily Small
Chloe the Kitten
Fairy Animals of Misty Wood

Lily Small
Bella the Bunny
Fairy Animals of Misty Wood

Lily Small
Paddy the Puppy
Fairy Animals of Misty Wood

Lily Small
Mia the Mouse
Fairy Animals of Misty Wood

Lily Small
Hailey the Hedgehog
Fairy Animals of Misty Wood

Lily Small
Poppy the Pony
Fairy Animals of Misty Wood

Lily Small
Sophie the Squirrel
Fairy Animals of Misty Wood

Lily Small
Betsy the Bunny
Fairy Animals of Misty Wood

Lily Small
Daisy the Deer
Fairy Animals of Misty Wood

Lily Small
Katie the Kitten
Fairy Animals of Misty Wood

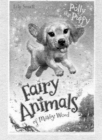

Lily Small
Polly the Puppy
Fairy Animals of Misty Wood

Lily Small
Paige the Pony
Fairy Animals of Misty Wood

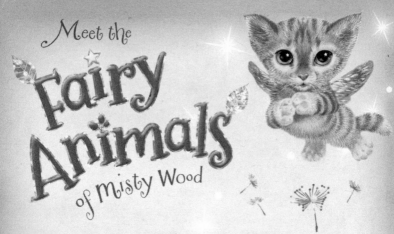

Meet the

Fairy Animals

of misty Wood

There's a whole world to explore!

Download the FREE *Fairy Animals* app and visit **fairyanimals.com** for lots of gorgeous goodies . . .

* Free stuff
* Games
* Write to your favourite characters
* Step inside Misty Wood
* Send us your cute pet pictures
* Make your own fairy wings!

Available on the
App Store